HORRiD HENRY'S
Christmas
Presents

Francesca Simon
Illustrated by Tony Ross

Orion
Children's Books

Horrid Henry's Christmas Presents originally appeared in
Horrid Henry's Christmas Cracker first published in
Great Britain in 2006 by Orion Children's Books
This edition first published in Great Britain in 2012
by Orion Children's Books
a division of the Orion Publishing Group Ltd
Orion House
5 Upper Saint Martin's Lane
London WC2H 9EA
An Hachette UK Company

7 9 10 8 6

ISBN 978 1 4440 0118 1
Printed in China

www.orionbooks.co.uk
www.horridhenry.co.uk

HORRiD HENRY'S
Christmas Presents

For Owen Sheers,
almost as good a poet as Horrid Henry.

Look out for . . .

Don't Be Horrid, Henry!
Horrid Henry's Birthday Party
Horrid Henry's Holiday
Horrid Henry's Underpants
Horrid Henry Gets Rich Quick
Horrid Henry and the Football Fiend
Horrid Henry's Nits
Horrid Henry and Moody Margaret
Horrid Henry's Thank You Letter
Horrid Henry Reads A Book
Horrid Henry's Car Journey
Moody Margaret's School
Horrid Henry Tricks and Treats
Horrid Henry's Christmas Play
Horrid Henry's Rainy Day
Horrid Henry's Author Visit
Horrid Henry Meets the Queen
Horrid Henry's Sports Day
Moody Margaret Casts a Spell

There are many more **Horrid Henry** books available.
For a complete list visit
www.horridhenry.co.uk

or

www.orionbooks.co.uk

 Contents

Chapter 1

Horrid Henry sat by the Christmas
tree and stuffed himself full of the
special sweets he'd nicked from the
special Christmas Day stash when
Mum and Dad weren't looking.

Horrid Henry was feeling delighted with himself and with the world. Granny and Grandpa, his grown-up cousins Pimply Paul and Prissy Polly, and their baby Vomiting Vera were coming to spend Christmas. Whoopee, thought Horrid Henry, because they'd all have to bring *him* presents.

Thankfully, Rich-Aunt Ruby and Stuck-Up Steve weren't coming. They were off skiing. Henry hadn't forgotten the dreadful lime green cardigan Aunt Ruby had given him last year.

And as much as he hated cousin
Polly, anyone was better than
Stuck-Up Steve, even someone
who squealed all the time and had
a baby who threw up on everyone.

Mum dashed into the sitting room,
wearing a flour-covered apron
and looking frantic.

Henry choked down his mouthful
of sweets.

"Right, who wants to decorate
the tree?' said Mum. She held out a
cardboard box brimming with tinsel
and gold and silver and blue baubles.

"Me!" said Henry.

"Me!" said Peter.

Chapter 2

Horrid Henry dashed to the box
and scooped up as many shiny
ornaments as he could.

"I want to put on the gold baubles,"
said Henry.

"I want to put on the tinsel,"
said Peter.

"Keep away from my side of
the tree," hissed Henry.

"You don't have a side," said Peter.

"Do too."

"Do not," said Peter.

"I want to put on the tinsel *and* the baubles," said Henry.

"But I want to do the tinsel," said Peter.

"Tough," said Henry, draping Peter in tinsel.

"Muuum!" wailed Peter.
"Henry's hogging all the decorations.
And he's putting tinsel on me."

"Don't be horrid, Henry," said
Mum. "Share with your brother."

Peter carefully wrapped blue tinsel
round the lower branches.

"Don't put it there," said Henry,
yanking it off.

Trust Peter to ruin his beautiful plan.

"Muuum!" wailed Peter.

"He's wrecking my design,"
screeched Henry. "He doesn't know
how to decorate a tree."

"But I wanted it there!" protested
Peter. "Leave my tinsel alone."

"You leave my stuff alone then,"
said Henry.

"He's wrecked my design!"
shrieked Henry and Peter.

Chapter 3

"Stop fighting, both of you!"
shrieked Mum.

"He started it!" screamed Henry.

"Did not!"

"Did too!"

"That's enough," said Mum.
"Now, whose turn is it to put the
fairy on top?"

"I don't want to have that stupid
fairy," wailed Horrid Henry.
"I want to have Terminator
Gladiator instead."

"No," said Peter. "I want the fairy.
We've always had the fairy."

"Terminator!"

"Fairy!"

"Terminator!"

"Fairy!"

Slap

Slap

"Waaaaaaa!"

"We're having the fairy," said Mum
firmly, "and I'll put it on the tree."

"Noooooo!"
screamed Henry.
"Why can't we do what
I want to do? I never get
to have what I want."

"Liar!" whimpered Peter.

"I've had enough of this," said Mum.
"Now get your presents and put
them under the tree."

Peter ran off.

Henry stood still.

"Henry," said Mum.
"Have you finished wrapping your
Christmas presents?"

Yikes, thought Horrid Henry.
What am I going to do now?

Chapter 4

The moment he'd been dreading
for weeks had arrived.

"Henry! I'm not going to ask
you again," said Mum.
"Have you finished wrapping all
your Christmas presents?"

"Yes!" bellowed Horrid Henry.
This was not entirely true.
Henry had not finished wrapping his
Christmas presents. In fact, he hadn't
even started. The truth was, Henry
had finished wrapping because he
had no presents to wrap.

This was certainly *not* his fault.
He *had* bought a few gifts, certainly.
He knew Peter would love the box
of green Day-Glo slime.
And if he didn't, well, he knew
who to give it to.

And Granny and Grandpa and
Mum and Dad and Paul and Polly
would have adored the big boxes of
chocolates Henry had won at the
school fair.

Could he help it if the chocolates had called his name so loudly that he'd been forced to eat them all?

And then Granny had been
complaining about gaining weight.
Surely it would have been very
unkind to give her chocolate.

And eating chocolate would have just
made Pimply Paul's pimples worse.

Henry had done him a big favour
eating that box.

And it was hardly Henry's fault when he'd needed extra goo for a raid on the Secret Club and Peter's present was the only stuff to hand.

He'd meant to buy replacements.

But he had so many things he needed to buy for himself that when he opened his skeleton money bank to get out some cash for Christmas shopping, only 35p had rolled out.

"I've bought and wrapped all my presents, Mum," said Perfect Peter. "I've been saving my pocket money for months."

"Whoopee for you," said Henry.

"Henry, it's always better to give than to receive," said Peter.

Mum beamed. "Quite right, Peter."

"Says who?" growled Horrid Henry. "I'd much rather get presents."

"Don't be so horrid, Henry," said Mum.

"Don't be so selfish, Henry," said Dad.

Horrid Henry stuck out his tongue.
Mum and Dad gasped.

"You horrid boy," said Mum.

"I just hope Father Christmas didn't
see that," said Dad.

"Henry," said Peter,
"Father Christmas won't bring you
any presents if you're bad."

Aaarrrgghhh!

Horrid Henry sprang at Peter.
He was a grizzly bear guzzling
a juicy morsel.

"Aaaaiieee," wailed Peter. "Henry pinched me."

"Henry! Go to your room," said Mum.

"Fine!" screamed Horrid Henry, stomping off and slamming the door.

Why did he get stuck with
the world's meanest and most
horrible parents?
They certainly didn't deserve
any presents.

Chapter 5

Presents!
Why couldn't he just *get* them?
Why oh why did he have to
give them?

Giving other people presents was such a waste of his hard-earned money. Every time he gave a present it meant something he couldn't buy for himself.

Goodbye chocolate.

Goodbye comics.

Goodbye Deluxe Goo-Shooter.

And then, if you bought
anything good, it was so horrible
having to give it away.
He'd practically cried having to give
Ralph that Terminator Gladiator
poster for his birthday.

And the Mutant Max lunchbox
Mum had made him give Kasim
still made him gnash his teeth
whenever he saw Kasim with it.

Now he was stuck,
on Christmas Eve, with no money,
and no presents to give anyone,
deserving or not.

And then Henry had a wonderful,
spectacular idea. It was so wonderful,
and so spectacular, that he couldn't
believe he hadn't thought of it
before.

Who said he had to *buy* presents?
Didn't Mum and Dad always say it
was the *thought* that counted?
And oh boy was he thinking.

Chapter 6

Granny was sure to love a Mutant
Max comic. After all, who wouldn't?
Then when she'd finished enjoying
it, he could borrow it back.

Horrid Henry rummaged under his
bed and found a recent copy.
In fact, it would be a shame if
Grandpa got jealous of Granny's
great present. Safer to give them each
one, thought Henry, digging deep
into his pile to find one with the
fewest torn pages.

Now let's see, Mum and Dad.
He could draw them a lovely picture.
Nah, that would take too long.
Even better, he could write them
a poem.

Henry sat down at his desk,
grabbed a pencil, and wrote:

Dear Old baldy Dad
Don't be sad
    Be glad
Because you've had...
A very merry Christmas
    Love from your lad,
        Henry

Not bad, thought Henry. Not bad.
And so cheap! Now one for Mum.

Dear Old wrinkly Mum
Don't be glum
Cause you've got a fat tum
And an even bigger bum
Ho ho ho hum
Love from your son,

Henry

Wow! It was hard finding so many words to rhyme with mum but he'd done it. And the poem was nice and Christmassy with the "ho ho ho".

Son didn't rhyme but hopefully Mum
wouldn't notice because she'd be
so thrilled with the rest of the poem.
When he was famous she'd be proud
to show off the poem her son
had written specially for her.

Now, Polly. Hmmmn.
She was always squeaking and
squealing about dirt and dust.
Maybe a lovely kitchen sponge?

Or a rag she could use to mop up
after Vera?

Or a bucket to put over
Pimply Paul's head?

Wait. What about some soap?

Horrid Henry nipped into the
bathroom. Yes! There was a
tempting bar of blue soap going
to waste in the soap dish by the
bathtub.

True, it had been used once or
twice, but a bit of smoothing with
his fingers would sort that out.
Polly and Paul could share this
present, it was such a good one.

Whistling, Horrid Henry wrapped up
the soap in sparkling reindeer paper.

He was a genius.
Why hadn't he ever done this
before?

Chapter 7

A lovely rag from under the sink
would be perfect as a gag for Vera.

That just left Peter and all his present
problems would be over.
A piece of chewing gum,
only one careful owner?

A collage of sweet wrappers which
spelled out *Worm*?

The unused comb Peter had given *him* last Christmas?

Aha. Peter loved bunnies.
What better present than a picture
of a bunny?

It was the work of a few moments
for Henry to draw a bunny and
slash a few blue lines across it to
colour it in. Then he signed his
name in big letters at the bottom.

Maybe he should be a famous artist
and not a poet when he grew up,
he thought, admiring his handiwork.

Henry had heard that artists got paid loads of cash just for stacking a few bricks or hurling paint at a white canvas. Being an artist sounded like a great job, since it left so much time for playing computer games.

Horrid Henry dumped his presents
beneath the Christmas tree and
sighed happily.
This was one Christmas where
he was sure to get a lot more than
he gave.

Whoopee! Who could ask for
anything more?